Published by Top That! Publishing plc
Tide Mill Way, Woodbridge, Suffolk, IP12 1AP, UK
www.topthatpublishing.com
Illustration copyright © Rebecca Elliott 2010
Text copyright © Rebecca Elliott 2010
All rights reserved
0 2 4 6 8 9 7 5 3 1
Printed and bound in China

Creative Director—Simon Couchman
Editorial Director—Daniel Graham

Written and illustrated by Rebecca Elliott

ISBN 978-1-84956-886-9

Printed and bound in China

Cub's First Winter

by Rebecca Elliott

"For Mum and Dad who have always taken such good care of their own cubs. x"

It was the first day of winter
and Cub could not sleep. "OK," said Mom.
"One more forest walk before bed. Come on..."

"Why are all the trees undressed?" asked Cub.

"So that we can have
fun in the leaves!"
answered Mom.

And the snow clouds
gathered in the sky.

"Why are my friends asleep
all the time?" asked Cub.
"Ssshhh! So that we can
laugh at their snoring!"
giggled Mom.

And the first snowflake fell to the ground.

"Why are the birds
going on vacation?" asked Cub.
"So they can tell us all about their
journey when they come back!" said Mom.

And the snow began to gently fall.

"Why is it so windy?" asked Cub.
"So that we can be blown about together
in the tall grass!" laughed Mom.

And the snow drifted down.

"Why can I see my own breath?" asked Cub.
"So that we can puff like steam trains!" puffed Mom.

And the snow began to settle on the ground.

"Why is the river solid?" asked Cub.
"So that we can slide and dance on it!"
exclaimed Mom.

And the snow fell more quickly.

"Why does the sun disappear
so early?" asked Cub.
"So that we can look up at
the stars for longer,"
explained Mom.

And the snow got
deeper and deeper.

"Why is everything white?" asked Cub.

"Oh no!" gasped Mom.
"Quick, follow me before we lose our way home!"

And back they went through the white forest,
over the white river, up and down the white rocks
and around and around the white trees until,
at last, they found their way home!

"Why is it so c-c-cold?"
asked Cub.

"So that we can
snuggle up tight,"
whispered Mom,
with a smile.

"Why am I so tired?"
yawned Cub.
"Because it is sleepy time,"
murmured Mom.
"Night, night little cub."